Born Yesterday

THE DIARY OF A young JOURNALIST

James Solheim • illustrated by Simon James

PHILOMEL BOOKS • AN IMPRINT OF PENGUIN GROUP (USA) INC.

for Jenny and Justin (my young editorial assistants),
and for Joyce, who makes it all possible,
and for Courtenay Palmer,
whose commitment and great ideas brought this book into being.
—J. S.

Philomel Books

A division of Penguin Young Readers Group. Published by The Penguin Group.
Penguin Group (USA) Inc., 375 Hudson Street, New York, NY 10014, U.S.A.
Penguin Group (Canada), 90 Eglinton Avenue East, Suite 700, Toronto, Ontario M4P 2Y3, Canada
(a division of Pearson Penguin Canada Inc.).
Penguin Books Ltd, 80 Strand, London WC2R 0RL, England.
Penguin Ireland, 25 St. Stephen's Green, Dublin 2, Ireland (a division of Penguin Books Ltd).
Penguin Group (Australia), 250 Camberwell Road, Camberwell, Victoria 3124, Australia
(a division of Pearson Australia Group Pty Ltd).
Penguin Books India Pvt Ltd, 11 Community Centre, Panchsheel Park, New Delhi - 110 017, India.
Penguin Group (NZ), 67 Apollo Drive, Rosedale, North Shore 0632, New Zealand (a division of Pearson New Zealand Ltd).
Penguin Books (South Africa) (Pty) Ltd, 24 Sturdee Avenue, Rosebank, Johannesburg 2196, South Africa.
Penguin Books Ltd, Registered Offices: 80 Strand, London WC2R 0RL, England.

Published simultaneously in Canada. Manufactured in China by South China Printing Co. Ltd.
Design by Ryan Thomann. Text set in Paradigm. The illustrations are rendered in watercolor and ink.

Library of Congress Cataloging-in-Publication Data
Solheim, James. Born yesterday : the diary of a young journalist / James Solheim ; illustrated by Simon James. p. cm.
Summary: A baby who plans to grow up to be a writer records thoughts and events in a private journal.
[1. Babies—Fiction. 2. Diaries—Fiction. 3. Humorous stories.] I. James, Simon, 1961– ill. II. Title.
PZ7.S689Bo 2010   [E]—dc22   2009006251
ISBN 978-0-399-25155-9
Special Markets ISBN 978-0-399-25558-8 Not for resale
3 5 7 9 10 8 6 4

Born Yesterday

THE DIARY OF A young JOURNALIST

James Solheim • illustrated by Simon James

PHILOMEL BOOKS • AN IMPRINT OF PENGUIN GROUP (USA) INC.

July 7th

Talk about unexpected.

I was in the dark, thinking about my future career as a writer, when suddenly I was in this cold pan and a lady was rubbing me all over with a towel.

I wasn't wearing so much as a hair ribbon. And horror! My mom and dad were there.

If I'd known I was going to be born in public, I'd at least have put on a tank top.

July 9th

Met my big sister for the first time today.

She is like some kind of monkey-bar superstar or something!

She can do all kinds of unbelievable things, like

- flip
- skip
- keep a bug running in circles in her macaroni dinner
- and put on her shirt so the buttons line up (almost).

Note to myself: Imitate that girl. Just imitate her.

Every second of every day, be just like her. But first—learn to roll over.

August 18th

I keep wanting to bat at this thingy hanging over my crib.
I don't know what it is about that thingy. I mean, it's only a
green star shape on a string, but it twirls and sparkles
and *taunts* me.

    I wave at it.
And miss.
    I wave at it.
I miss again.
    I try and try and
yet I can't hit it.

My sister can hit it. Plus, she
has her very own hairbrush and
mosquito bite. Me, I have exactly
zero hairbrushes.

    That is so unfair. I have a hair, too!

September 8th

I'm not sure what kindergarten is, but to get in, I think kids have to make mud pies. The mayor chooses the best pies, and the winning kids get to be kindergartners.

My sister already is a kindergartner, so she must be really talented! (Or she knows someone important, like the bus driver.)

Kindergartners get to study advanced subjects like

- pasta art
- Friendship Corner
- and the hardest one of all: sitting still for a full minute with hands folded.

I heard my sister is the only one who can do that.
And she can play a harmonica with her eyes shut,
an Important Life Skill.

October 28th

My big sister took me to see the world today.

(I hate to admit this, but I'd thought there were only a couple of places on Earth. Maybe three or four, tops.)

But my sister, she is like this worldly super-chick that knows *everything*!

She knows where the leaves are that can tickle.

She knows where the best anthills are and how to operate a Popsicle. She even let me take a lick.

I think she may secretly be a genius.

November 1st

Guess what!

    My hands can do more than just write. They can grab things!

    I made a mental list of things to grab:

- cats
- ears
- elephants
- ankles
- Vermont

On the subject of ankles: I didn't realize they were part of me. So I bit one.

    Ow!

    Good thing nobody was looking. My reputation would be *so* ruined!

November 14th

Today my sister pushed my stroller. Along with some spit bubbles,
I made sounds: "Take me to Fun World. Fun World!"

But she just kept pushing me
to her junky old piano lesson.

"Fun World. Fun World,"
I whispered.

She shoved a big
pink bunny into my face.

Oooh, soft! I giggled
up some more spit bubbles.
I grabbed and wrestled and
hugged that big old bunny!

Then I realized.
She wanted me to
forget about Fun World.
But no. Fun World is my
dream! That and getting
hold of the fuzzy ear thing
next to my face.

January 6th

Nobody has told me this for sure,
but I think people grow.

So I keep looking at my hand.
I put my fist in my mouth, trying
to feel sprouting teeth. Nothing.

Everybody else gets old, drinks lemonade,

answers the phone, runs the seven-minute mile.

I do nothing except spit up.

I must focus. Focus!

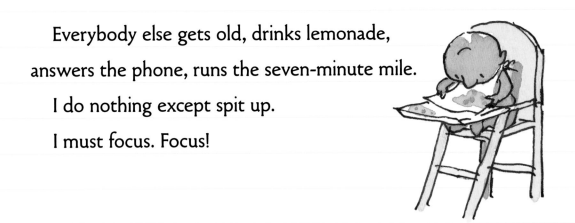

Up, down, up, down. Fling that food, make it fly.

With my new high-chair workout,

I plan to be big by Friday.

February 23rd

Why is nobody taking me to school?
Ever since I was born, it's like
they've been avoiding the subject.
I mean, come *on*!
My sister gets to go to school.
My babysitter gets to go to school.

Even my dog
Foofy goes to school.

If this goes on much longer, I will have to contact the mayor.

March 22nd

Finally—I have it figured out. Some things are noses, some are taxicabs, and some are Belgians. The up end of people is their hairstyles and the down end is their tootsie-wootsies.

These tootsie-wootsie things are fascinating. I plan to write a book about them.

My sister paints her tootsie-wootsie nails a special color called striped. I can't wait till I can paint my tootsie-wootsie nails the color called striped, and thus become a super-chick person like my sister.

For now, I just lift them to my mouth and suck.

Boys are similar to people, except they make funny sounds. When this boy item came to visit, my sister ignored me almost forever. So I banged on my crib.

But my sister still smiled at this boy item. And blurted out that she once ate a cricket. He answered with the loudest burp in history. It was obvious they liked each other.

I started to wail. My sister ignored me even worse.

Note to myself: Wailing does not work. Try wheedling.

My sister tells Foofy everything. *And* gives him half her
doughnut holes.

Me, she tells nothing. All I get is a pacifier, which is this
pretend food on a ring. As if I won't notice it's fake. Hey, Sis—
do I look like some kind of naïve newborn or something?

When I grow up to be a Famous Author, my sister will
be sorry. I will write my own commercials, starring her as
Miss Mouthwash, the Queen of Bad Breath.

May 20th

Tragedy!
My sister has
read my diary.

I am so embarrassed. Worse than embarrassed.
I may just be a Jell-O head by morning.

As soon as I saw her
reading it, I shut my eyes
tight—pretend tight, that
is. I left one eye open just
enough to watch her.

She laughed and
laughed at my collected
writings, then shook her
head at me. I could only cry.

I guess I'm not her
friend like Foofy is. She
never laughs at Foofy.

Maybe I'll take a job
as a baby in a different
family. If I could just roll
close enough to the front
door to hail a cab . . .

May 22nd

When my sister came home from school today, *she* was the one crying.

Big battling gasps of air.
Monster hiccups of sorrow.

She crawled into my crib and held me. She said,
"You always listen, and you only laugh *with* me, not *at* me.
You are my best friend."

Me? Her best friend? This was amazing news.
I was so relieved that I tried to eat her hair.

June 30th

We have started a club. It's called Young Authors
of the World. So far, the club has only three people in it—
me, my sister, and Foofy.

Foofy is club president.

The three of us made a pact:

to stay best friends forever. For *Ever*.

Which is all I really wanted.

Well, that and to climb Mount Everest.

But first I have to figure out

how to climb out of this playpen. . . .